2 95

The Desert People

Also by Ann Nolan Clark

The Desert People

BY ANN NOLAN CLARK

ILLUSTRATED BY ALLAN HOUSER

4283

The Viking Press

New York

For

Phoebe and Carl

The Desert People

I am a boy
   of the Desert People.

White men call me Indian.
White men call me Papago
   but the wild animals
   call me Brother
   because they know me
   and love me.

We call ourselves
   the Desert People.

I live in a village
    in the desert country,
    the flat sand country,
    the hot dry country.

Purple mountains fence it.
Hot winds sweep it.
Heat mist fills it
    and above us
    hangs the empty
    turquoise sky.

My village is here
    in the desert.

The name of my village is
    Place-Where-Waters-Meet.

In the Rainy Moon,
    when the rains pour down,
    rain waters run
    to the dry-wash there,
    overflowing its banks
    to give our thirsty fields
    rain water to drink.

12

It is good to live
　　at Place-Where-Waters-Meet.

My village has houses
　　of ocotillo and cactus ribs.
It has no streets.

Each house has a yard
　　fenced with cactus ribs
　　and swept
　　clean and bare.

Each house has a ramada
　　made of mesquite posts
　　and roofed with branches.

In the ramada
　　are the bedrolls
　　of the family
　　for night sleeping.
Hanging from the roof poles
　　is the water olla
　　damp and cool.

The houses of my village
   belong to my father
   and to my uncles
   and to my uncles' sons.

We live here together,
   the men and the boys,
   the women and the girls,
   in peace and happiness,
   with laughter and song.

My village has a Rain House,
   round-shaped,
   branch-covered,
   a holy place.

To the Rain House
   each night
   the men may go
   to make Song Magic.

Women and children
   sit outside.
They may hear the songs.
They may not sing them.

It is good
   to be a boy
   of the Desert People.
I am happy
   and proud.

We have ways
   of doing things
   that have been given
   to us

16

by Desert People
who have gone
    before us.

These ways are our ways.
We must not forget them.
We must not change them.
We must follow them.
They are the footsteps
    of our Ancients.

We have our ways
    of doing things.
We have a pattern
    for our days.

In the morning-gray dawn
    I hear my father
    talking to us
    where we are sleeping
    in the ramada.
He is telling us
    the things
    that we should know.

My father says,
"We are Desert People.
We must be swift.
We must be brave.
We must be men.

"Sometimes
     we are hungry and thirsty,
     we are sunburned and tired,
     but we must meet these things
     without words
     that cry out
     to shame us."

My father says,
"These things are not given us.
We learn to know them
     by many meetings.
Morning stands up, my sons.
Stand up to meet it.
Go forth into the dawn,
     running."

It is always this way.

When morning stands up,
   my father wakens us
   with low-voice talking
   made of good words.

All our days
   begin with this pattern,
   but the work
   of each day changes
   with the changes
   that new moons bring
   to the desert
   and the things
   of the desert.

Now is the time
   of the Dry Grass Moon.

The wild plants and grasses
   in the hot, dry sands
   bend heavy heads downward,
   getting ready for sleep.

Now is the time
   of the Dry Grass Moon.

We drive our cattle
to the Town Market Place
and sell what we can
to the Cattle Buyers.

22

We sing to our herds
   as we drive them along.
We sing to them so
   they will not become frightened.

What we do not sell
  we drive to winter pasture
  in the purple mountains
  where there is water
  and grass.

We sing to our herds
  as we drive them along.
We sing to them so
  they will not become lonely.

The moon grows old.
A new moon comes.
Now is the time
  of the Harvest Moon.

In the fields
  the tasseled corn whispers.
The melons lie heavy.
The bean pods are flat and green.
The squash are fat and yellow
  and the red chili flames.

Now is the time
  of the Harvest Moon.

In the fields
　　the men cut the cornstalks
　　and pile them.
They pick the beans and chili,
　　the squash and melons,
　　and put them into piles
　　for the women.
They clean the fields.
This is men's work.

The women carry the loads
　　of cornstalks and beans,
　　chili, melon, and squash
　　to their house yards
　　to shell them and string them,
　　to cut them and dry them
　　for winter's food.
This is women's work.

The moon grows old.
A new moon comes.
Now is the time
　　of the Small-Winter Moon.

The wind blows over the sand,
   swaying the dry grass,
   chasing the whirlwinds.
We go inside our houses
   and light the center fire.

Now is the time
   of the Small-Winter Moon.

Now that thunder sleeps
    it is safe to hear
    the stories the Old Men tell.

They tell of Elder Brother
    who lives on top
    of Holy Mountain
    and who holds
    in his hands
    the rainbow ribbons
    of the trail-ways
    of the Desert People.

They tell us the Secrets
    of the Desert People
    that only the Desert People
    may know.

My father listens,
    but I can not see
    his face
    because the smoke
    of the center fire
    curls above him
    in blue clouds,

hiding his face
and his thoughts.

But he listens.
My father listens
   to the Old Men's words.

My mother listens
   as she weaves
   her willow basket.
In the firelight
   I see her fingers
   like swift birds flying
   and singing for me

the song in her heart.

My big brother listens.
I can feel him listening.
He looks at the firelight
    and his eyes are filled
    with dreams.

31

The moon grows old.
A new moon comes.
Now is the time
   of the Big-Winter Moon.

The sun smiles down
   on the dusty desert.
Heat waves and whirlwinds
   play games
   on the flat land.
A gray wind sings
   in the dry grass
   and hums a tune
   in the cactus spines.

Now is the time
   of the Big-Winter Moon.

Big-Winter Moon
   is time for Fiesta,
   for dancing and feasting
   and roping and singing
   and being a cowboy,
   yipi ye, yipi ye.

We put on our best clothes
   and go in our wagons
   to the church
   at the Mission
   to have a Fiesta
   to honor its Saints.

Yipi ye, yipi ye,
   yipi ye.

We dance Spanish dances
   and Mexican dances
   and we whirl and we twirl
   and we stamp and we clap,
   yipi ye, yipi ye,
   yipi ye.

We come to the church
at the old Spanish Mission
to honor its Saints.

34

The Old Men, too,
   honor the Saints.
They dance Indian dances,
   patting their feet
   on the warm sand
   before the church door.

They pound their basket drums
   with the flats of their hands
   like thunder pounding
   rain from the clouds.

Then we forget
   we are cowboys.
We are Indian again.
We are Papago again.
We are the People
   of the old, old Desert.

The moon grows old.
A new moon comes.
Now is the time
of the Deer Moon.

We go to the mountains
to watch the deer,
to learn their ways

and to tell them
that in this moon
we never hunt them.

Deer are our Brothers.
They take care of us.
This has been true
    since the Beginning.

The mountains are green
   with tall pines
   and sturdy oaks
   and lacy ferns.

The tops of the pines
   are misted in blue cloud.
Among the oak leaves
   hides blue shadow
   and the deer in the fern bed
   look at us.

By day, we watch them.
By starlight, we sing to them.
At night we sleep close
   to their hideaways.

The moon grows old.
A new moon comes.
Now is the time
   the Gray Moon comes.

The desert turns gray.
Plants have no leaves.
Their stems are gray.
The Giant Cactus grows
thin and old.

42

The sky is gray smoke.
The sand is gray dust.
The sun turns dull.

Gray Moon time
    comes to the desert.

The men of my village
    journey to the Big Waters
    of the Sea
    for salt.
This is a Holy Pilgrimage.

We go the long journey
    across an unmarked way
    through deep, heavy sand,
    shifting and sun-scorched
    before we come
    to the ever-moving,
    never-ending sea.

We bring salt
    back to the People
    and they bless us.

The moon changes.
Green Moon walks
   across the night sky
   and calls
   to the sleeping desert
   to waken.

Plant things send upward
   thin, green fingers,
   waving them skyward
   to beckon the rain.

This is the time
   of the new Green Moon.

In the purple mountains
   where the cattle graze
   new calves are born.

We hunt for them
   in the fern beds
   and the oak thickets
   where their mothers hid them.

We find them
   and sing to them
   that they may grow
   fat and strong
   and increase
   our herds.

47

The moon changes.
The old moon goes.
The new moon comes.

Now is the time
   of the Yellow Moon.
The desert is bright
   with yellow flowers.

Now is the time
   of the Yellow Moon.

The paloverde trees
   wrap themselves
   in a yellow mist
   of tiny flowers.

The creosote trees
   that grow in the desert
   as if they had been planted
   by careful hands,
   are bright with yellow flowers
   like overgrown stars
   that the wind has swept
   from a crowded night sky.

We go to the purple mountains,
   to a high mountain meadow
   where a wild-horse herd
   outruns the wind.

We go to rope
   the oldest colts
   to catch them and gentle them,
   to brand them and train them,
   to own them and ride them.

The moon changes.
Now is the time
   of the Hunger Moon.

The desert is sun-scorched.
The water holes are dry.
The air is dust-filled.
For many moons
   there has been no rain.

We have eaten the corn,
   the beans and chili,
   the melons and squash.

We have eaten the grass seeds,
   the mesquite beans,
   and the cactus fruits.

We go now
   to hunt the deer
   and the small game,
   saying to them,
"Brothers, give yourselves
   to us
   that we may live."

Hunger Moon seems to linger
   because it is a time
   of sadness,
   but at last it goes.

The time comes now
    of the Black-Seed Moon
    when seeds of wild plants
    are ripe and black,
    when seeds of wild plants
    are full of goodness
    to end our hunger.

Now is the time
    of the Black-Seed Moon.

From dawn till darkness
    the women go
    across the desert,
    across the flat land,
    across the dry washes,
    through the forests
    of Giant Cactus
    to the rocky foothills,
    to fill their burden baskets
    with the ripe black seeds.

The women dry the seeds
   and grind them into meal
   to bake in bread
   to end our hunger.

Then comes the time
  of the Rainy Moon.
Clouds blot
  the stars away.
The wind lies still.
Thunder pounds.

Lightning zigzags,
    cutting the sky in two
    and the rains pour down,
    pour down, pour down.

Now is the time
    of the Rainy Moon.

The mountain sides
   are running
   in waterfalls.
The mountain trails
   are deep in water.
The dry washes fill.
The rivers flood.

The wild plants
   come to life.
The old-men cactus
   grow young again
   as rain water fattens
   their ribs.

We drive our cattle
   down the mountain trails
   to the rain-filled desert,
   to the green-growing desert.

The cattle mill and bawl.
The horses neigh.
The People sing
   and the rain pours down.

This is the time
   of the Rainy Moon.

The rains keep on,
   keep on
   through the moon change.

The new moon comes
   across the rain-wet sky,
   across the rain-wet land.

The time of the Planting Moon
   comes to the Desert People.

We go to the Rain House
   to sing our Planting Songs.
The women and girls
   sit outside
   to listen.

We go to the fields
   with our pointed planting sticks.
We make the holes
   in the rain-wet sand.
The women and the girls
   drop the seeds
   into the shallow holes.

They drop the seeds
to our singing.

Thus the year ends.
It is finished.